MW00633620

Young People's Stories of Fairness

Fairness is...treating people the way you would like to be treated.

Fairness is...keeping the promises you make.

Fairness is...giving other people a chance.

Fairness is...returning favors and other kindnesses that people give you.

Fairness is...valued by people around the world.

Compiled by
Henry and Melissa Billings

Young People's Press
San Diego

Editorial, design and production by
Book Production Systems, Inc.

Cover illustration by David Wenzel.

Published in the United States of America.

3 4 5 6 7 8 9 – 99 98 97 96
ISBN 1-885658-07-9

Young People's Stories of Fairness

This story comes from Italy. It is based on a tale written nearly 700 years ago. The story tells how a judge is faced with a difficult problem and how he solves it with fairness.

THE WISE JUDGE

Many years ago there lived a man named Sir Rubaconte. He was known to all for being very fair. When he was made a judge, everyone cheered.

One day a difficult case was brought
to his court. The case involved Bagnai, a
good but unlucky man. One day Bagnai was
crossing a bridge. Suddenly he saw a group
of young horsemen galloping wildly toward
him. Bagnai was terrified.

To save himself from being trampled
to death, Bagnai jumped onto the railing of
the bridge. But he slipped. He fell into the
river. He landed on a woman who
was sitting on the bank
washing her feet. Bagnai
fell with such force
that the woman was
instantly killed.

The family of the woman wanted Bagnai punished. So they came to Sir Rubaconte.

"Judge," they said, "we ask that you sentence Bagnai to death. After all, the law says that anyone who commits a murder must himself be put to death."

Sir Rubaconte knew that this was true. But he also knew that Bagnai had not murdered the woman on purpose. Bagnai had killed her accidentally, through no fault of his own. This, Sir Rubaconte knew, was different.

The judge tried to convince the family of the difference. But they only yelled more loudly. They demanded that the letter of the law be followed. How else, they cried, could people ever again wash their feet by the bank of a quiet river in peace and safety?

Meanwhile, Bagnai stood there silently. He was confused by all the shouting. He was badly bruised by his fall. Sir Rubaconte was determined to save this gentle, unfortunate man.

At last Sir Rubaconte gave his ruling. He said that Bagnai should go sit in the very place where the woman had been sitting. The woman's brother—who had yelled most loudly—should climb up onto the bridge. Another relative should push him off so that he would be sure to fall directly on Bagnai. This, Sir Rubaconte said, would be fair.

The brother thought about the height
of the bridge. He thought about the cold
waters of the river. He looked at the bruised
and battered Bagnai and thought about the
damage that the fall would do to his body.
Without a word, he turned and left the
court. The rest of the family followed.

A cheer arose from the courtroom as Bagnai thanked the wise judge for such a fair judgment.

Sir Rubaconte knew it would not be fair simply to sentence Bagnai to death. Bagnai had not intended to kill anyone. Bagnai himself had suffered in the accident. Still, Sir Rubaconte had to be fair to the woman's family. His ruling allowed the family to kill the "murderer" but only if they were willing to suffer as Bagnai had suffered. As the judge expected, the family was not willing to do this.

Señor Coyote
Settles a Quarrel

This story comes from Mexico. It tells what can happen when someone does not treat others with fairness.

One morning the Rattlesnake crawled out of his den. He lay down at the foot of a mountain and fell asleep. While he was sleeping, a large rock came loose from the side of the mountain. It rolled to the bottom. It stopped right on top of Señor Rattlesnake.

Señor Rattlesnake awoke and found himself pinned to the ground. He twisted and squirmed, grunted and stretched. But he could not escape. Then he heard footsteps hopping down the canyon.

"Who could this be?" thought the Snake. "Certainly not one of my friends. I have none."

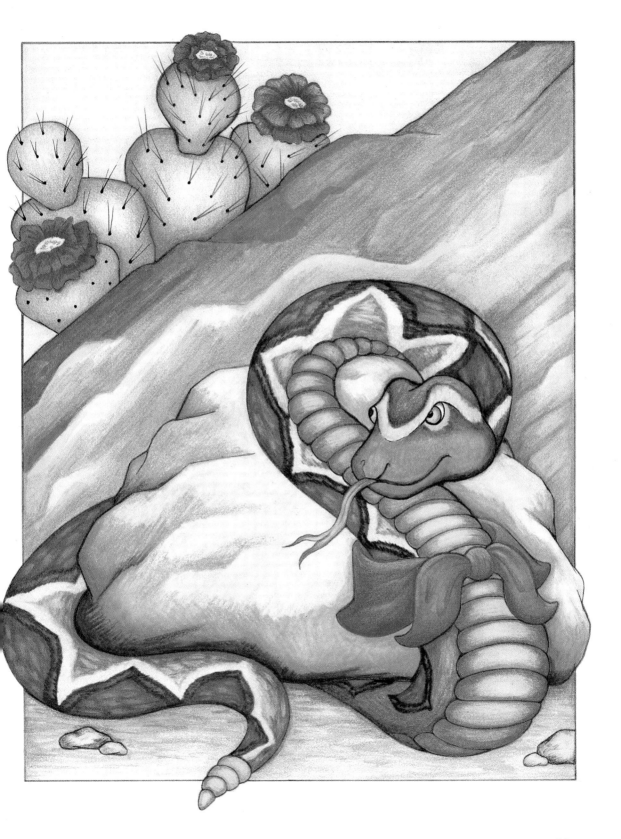

In a moment here came Señor Conejo
(Mr. Rabbit).

"Help me! Help me! Brother Rabbit,"
called the Snake from under the rock. "Help
me and I will see that you are well rewarded."

The Rattlesnake began to groan as if
he were about to die. Rabbit was such a kind-
hearted animal that he hated to see even his
worst enemy in such trouble.

"Calm down, Brother Rattlesnake," said the little Rabbit. "I will get this rock off you somehow."

So the little Rabbit got a pole and put it under the stone. He braced himself on the side of the mountain. Then he lifted and pushed, over and over. Finally he rolled the heavy rock off the Rattlesnake.

"Now," said the Snake, "about your reward."

"Oh, that's all right," said the Rabbit. "I don't need a reward."

"But you haven't heard my plan," said the Snake with an evil grin.

"What do you mean?" asked the Rabbit, becoming frightened.

"I mean," said the Snake, "that your reward is that you will be my dinner."

At this moment the Coyote appeared. "What is going on here?" he asked.

"I helped the Snake," said the Rabbit. "I rolled this big stone off him, and now he wants to eat me as a reward."

"That is not true," said the Snake. "The Rabbit tried to roll the rock so that it would crush me worse than it had already."

The Coyote took off his big sombrero and scratched his head. "Let me think a minute," he said.

At last he said, "I tell you what we will do. Both of you go to the exact spot where

you were when Rabbit came along. Then I can
see just how things happened. That way I can
easily decide who is in the right."

So the Coyote and the Rabbit pushed
and shoved the rock back on the Snake. Then
the Rabbit went up the canyon and came hopping back down to the rock.

"Is this the way it was, Brother Snake?"
asked the Coyote.

"Yes, this is the way I was," said the
Snake, squirming and making a face. "Get
this rock off me right now."

"If that is the way you were," said the Coyote, "then that is the way you will stay. This is your reward for trying to eat Brother Conejo after he had treated you so kindly."

The Rattlesnake would have died without the Rabbit's help. Yet, after the Rabbit saved his life, all the Snake wanted to do was eat him. This clearly was not fair. The Coyote punished the Rattlesnake by leaving him exactly where he was before the Rabbit came along.

The Pied Piper of Hamelin

This story comes from Germany. It takes place in the town of Hamelin more than 700 years ago. It tells what happened when people broke their promise to a stranger.

A long time ago the town of Hamelin was invaded by rats. The rats ran all over the place. They attacked cats and dogs. They bit babies in their beds. It was hard to walk without stepping on a rat. The nasty little creatures were everywhere.

At last, the people got angry. "Something must be done!" they shouted to the mayor. But what? They tried several plans, but nothing worked. The rat problem just got worse.

Then one day, a stranger walked into town. He was an odd-looking fellow. He was tall and thin with deep, dark eyes. His nose was crooked. He wore funny clothes that were all colors of the rainbow. The stranger also had a string around his neck. On it was a small pipe.

"People call me the Pied Piper," he announced to the mayor. "What are you willing to pay me if I get rid of all the rats?"

The town did not have much money. Still, something had to be done about the rats. So the mayor promised the Pied Piper one thousand gold coins if he could get rid of the rats.

"That sounds fair," said the Pied Piper.

The Pied Piper then stepped out into the street. He began to play his small pipe. It was a squeaky, scratchy song. The tune could be heard all over the town. For a moment nothing happened. Then the people of Hamelin heard a rumbling noise. It started low but grew louder and louder.

What was it? It was the rats! Every rat in Hamelin came tumbling out of its hole and onto the street. The rats rushed to where the Pied Piper stood. The Pied Piper, still tooting on his pipe, marched toward the river. The rats followed. When they reached the river, the rats kept marching straight ahead. One by one they tumbled into the river. Soon they were all washed down the stream, never to be seen again.

The people of Hamelin jumped for joy. "Hurrah for the Pied Piper!" they shouted.

Soon, however, the shouting died down. The mayor and the people began to think about the one thousand gold coins. That was a lot of money. In fact, they decided, it was *too much money*. The Pied Piper hadn't worked very hard. Anyone could have done what he did.

"We are safe now," said the mayor. "All the rats have drowned. But I do not believe the Pied Piper deserves one thousand gold coins. One gold coin should be enough."

The people of Hamelin agreed. The next day when the Pied Piper came to collect his money, the mayor handed him just one gold coin.

"This is not fair!" cried the Pied Piper angrily. "We made a deal. I lived up to my half of the bargain. You must live up to your half. If you don't," he added darkly, "there are other tunes I can play."

The mayor laughed. "Don't try to frighten us. What can you do? The rats are all dead. Go on your way."

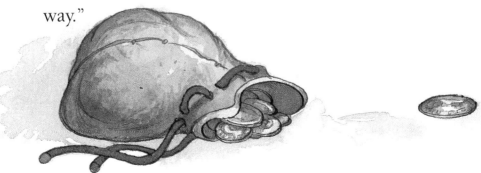

The Pied Piper's eyes narrowed. "Very well," he said coldly. "This is not the first time someone has broken a promise to me. It probably won't be the last."

He then put the pipe to his lips and began to play. This time it was a happy, cheerful tune. The people of Hamelin smiled. "The rats are all gone," they whispered. "Why is this silly fellow still playing his pipe?"

Soon, however, they saw a strange sight. The children of Hamelin came rushing out from houses, schools, and playgrounds. They marched up to the Pied Piper. The Piper turned and began walking out of town. He was still playing his happy song. The children marched after him. Their parents did not know what to do. They called after their children, but the children paid no attention.

27

The Pied Piper led the children through a
forest. Beyond it was a hill. When the Pied Piper
reached it, a door in the earth suddenly opened up.
All the children walked through the door. After the
last one marched through, the door shut tight. Then
there was only silence.

The townspeople searched for many, many days. But they never found the children. From that day to this, the people of Hamelin are careful never to break another promise.

As the story shows, breaking a promise is wrong. The mayor and the townspeople of Hamelin were not fair to the Pied Piper. He did what he promised. But they did not. The Pied Piper punished them by taking their children.

Acknowledgments

Grateful acknowledgment is made for permission to reprint the following copyrighted material:

"Señor Coyote Settles a Quarrel" from PICTURE TALES FROM MEXICO by Dan Storm, illustrated by Mark Storm. Copyright 1941 by Dan and Mark Storm. Reprinted by permission.